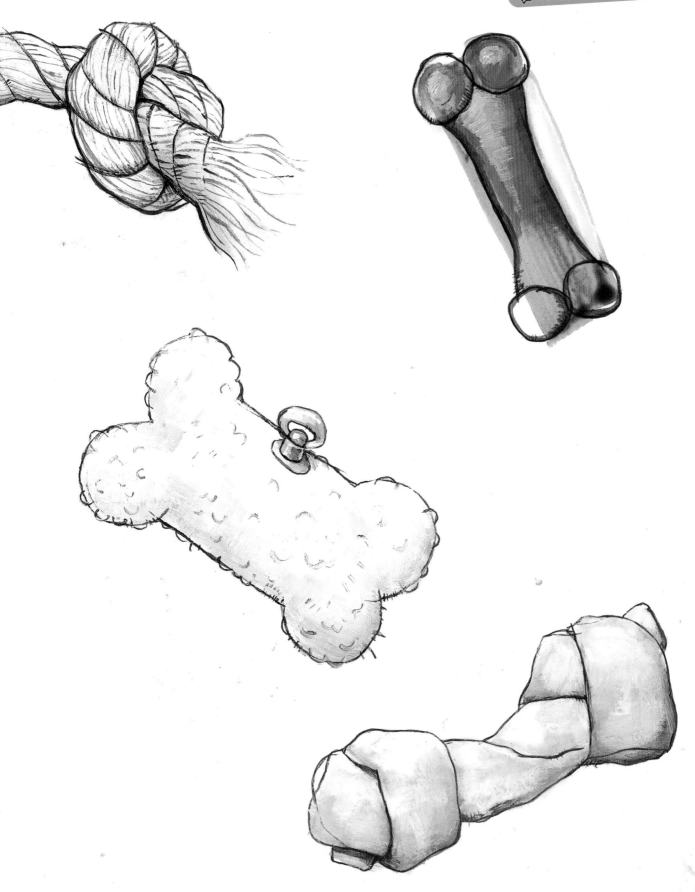

Good Boy, Fergus!

David Shannon

THE BLUE SKY PRESS

An Imprint of Scholastic Inc. • New York

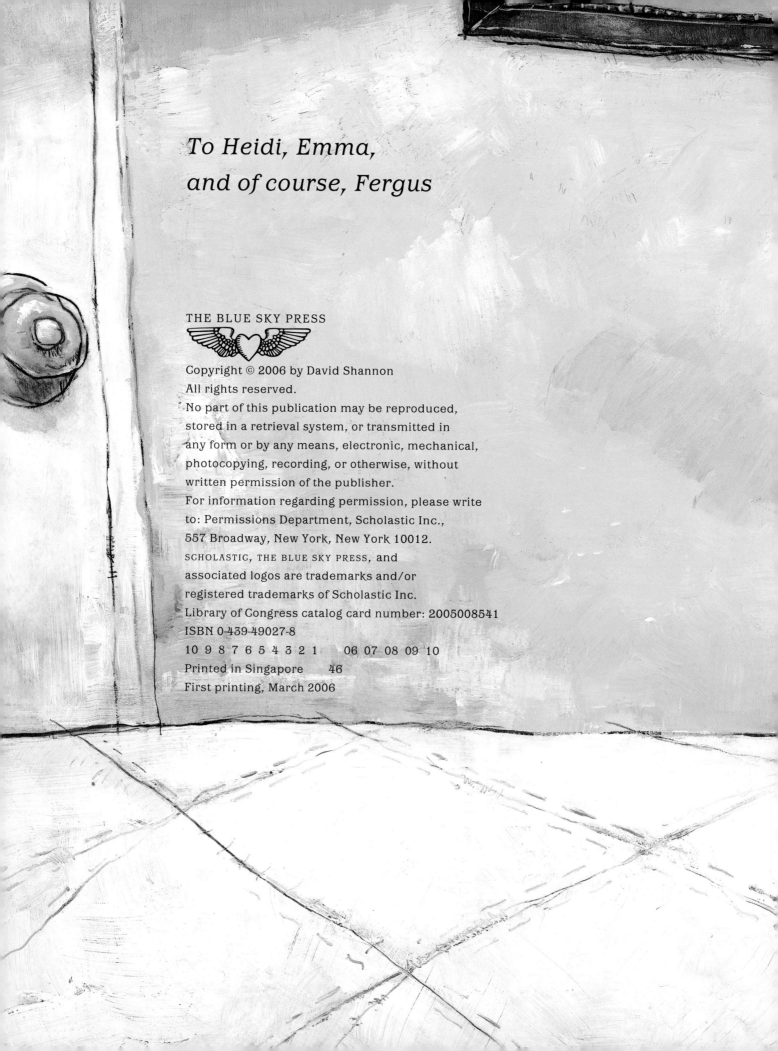

*To Heidi, Emma,
and of course, Fergus*

THE BLUE SKY PRESS

Copyright © 2006 by David Shannon
All rights reserved.
No part of this publication may be reproduced,
stored in a retrieval system, or transmitted in
any form or by any means, electronic, mechanical,
photocopying, recording, or otherwise, without
written permission of the publisher.
For information regarding permission, please write
to: Permissions Department, Scholastic Inc.,
557 Broadway, New York, New York 10012.
SCHOLASTIC, THE BLUE SKY PRESS, and
associated logos are trademarks and/or
registered trademarks of Scholastic Inc.
Library of Congress catalog card number: 2005008541
ISBN 0-439-49027-8
10 9 8 7 6 5 4 3 2 1   06 07 08 09 10
Printed in Singapore   46
First printing, March 2006

Ready...

set...

Okay, Fergie, time to go in. Come here, Ferg. C'mon boy. FERGUS, COME! Here Fe Fergie, Fergie! MACLAGGA HERE RIGHT NO Come on. Let's

It's
Mr. F!

Mister
itchy bobo
scratchitty
man!

Sit. Fergus.

Down.

Roll over.

Good boy, Fergus!

Bath time!

Now let's go for a ride!

Don't beg, Fergus.

Oh, all right...

Good boy, Fergus!

Time

for a walk?

t er?

Better!

Sweet dreams, little Fergus.

Good boy.

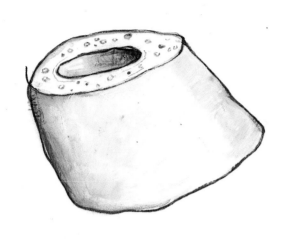

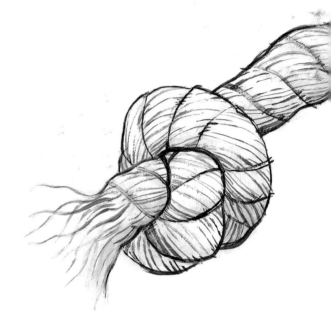

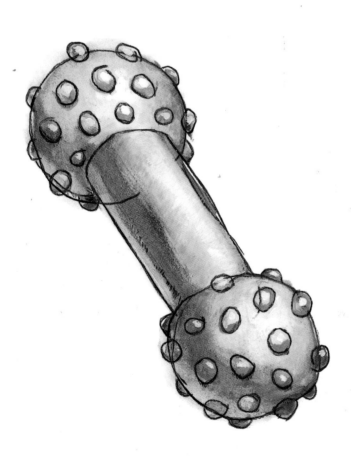

For my princesses of Strasbourg,
who lived together in a little atelier, drawing other princesses,
and sharing nice cake with a little prince inside...

This edition published by Parragon in 2010

Parragon
Queen Street House
4 Queen Street
Bath BA1 1HE, UK

Published by arrangement with Meadowside Children's Books, 185 Fleet Street, London EC4A 2HS.

ISBN 978-1-4454-0279-6

Printed in China